Love in the Time of Hate

Love in the Time of Hate

Diary of a Participant Observer

SUSANA PORRAS

Foreword by Anastascia Duchesse

RESOURCE *Publications* • Eugene, Oregon

Resource Publications
An Imprint of Wipf and Stock Publishers
199 W. 8th Ave., Suite 3
Eugene, OR 97401

www.wipfandstock.com

PAPERBACK ISBN: 979-8-3852-5421-7
HARDCOVER ISBN: 979-8-3852-5422-4
EBOOK ISBN: 979-8-3852-5423-1

07/08/25

To my Sweetheart, whose *risa* echoes in every word, and whose *amor* is the greatest *historia* I could tell.

Contents

Foreword

Pasadena will always hold an extraordinary place in my heart.

As a native San Diegan (by way of Texas!) I can't claim to have grown up there, but I found solace there after college, and shortly after two crucial pre-pandemic years I resided in France, years that would permanently alter my life (and hypothetically lead to me writing this now!).

My very first encounter with Pasadena was a vibrant "meet-cute" when a group of college friends corralled me there in a pair of pointed neon pumps for a ladies' night out. When it came time to find a SoCal apartment after teaching English in Europe for two years, I remembered those good vibes and proudly chose Pasadena as my home.

I was an emerging author at the time, having already written most of my debut novel[1] during my stint overseas but struggling to find the valor and sustenance to finish the "urban fiction adventure" inspired by my deeply transformative experiences living abroad as a Black American. When I wasn't deep into editing, I was out and about exploring the multicultural influences inherent in Pasadena's population and restaurants; authentic Italian kitchens,

---

1. The story rights to Anastascia's debut novel were acquired by Universal Television in October 2024. It has always been her dream to share her deeply personal journey of "transformation through travel" on-screen and inspire the masses to step outside their comfort zones. Duchesse, *Dabresha Goes to France*, 1–323.

savory Nepalese cuisine, classy vegan bistros, a decorative high tea house, and Yucatán-style botanas were all within walking distance from the main boulevard. Being surrounded by so many other creatives was magnetic and inspired me to persist on my writing path even as my cushy office jobs tempted me to stay in the "safe zone" of career ventures, where benefits, salary, and 401(k) options are guaranteed.

Along this early authoring journey, I crossed paths with Susana when I expressed to our mutual friend—a prominent figure in the city's administration—my disappointment at the lack of authors of color at a city-led book event. Susana so graciously addressed my concerns, inviting me to coffee and macarons at a local French-style bakery to discuss the matter. I did not expect the casual meeting would lend an opportunity to practice speaking *Français* and gain a new friend.

My first conversation with Susana was as bubbly as my favorite French rosé. We discovered a mutual appreciation for languages and cultures and bonded over living in the south of France at pivotal points in our young adulthood. She had the personality I've always gravitated towards "post-passport": open-minded yet assertive, health-conscious but unafraid to indulge in a few carbs. Poised and adventurous, the type to embrace any travel opportunity if circumstances permitted. I've booked international flights literally forty-eight hours before departure—and wouldn't be surprised if Susana has done the same!

As my friendship with Susana deepened, I realized that France had become a place we individually retreated to whenever we needed reflection time or a rapid reset from the hustle and bustle of "LA life," domestic life, work life, family life—or anything that wasn't quite right in our personal worlds at that moment. France is just a ten-hour flight away, ready to heal us, spiritually rejuvenate us, or reignite our nostalgia for artistic pastries, leisure-paced living, harmonious accordion music, medieval architecture, and double-cheeked *bisous* greetings. My most recent visit in October 2023—a nine-day solo trip to Cassis with incredible views of the Mediterranean coast from the lodging—helped me gain clarity and strength after a tumultuous postpartum experience. I'm sure the familiarity of knowing how to easily immerse ourselves in vastly different environments helped both Susana and me to individually navigate life's letdowns and similarly nurtured our respective accolades. It is a perpetual gift to be able to mentally whisk ourselves to serene overseas destinations at any moment without booking airfare.

Unsurprisingly, Susana and I have each launched creative careers that draw heavily from the international experiences—both fond and flawed—that have shaped and guided the paths we each walk as "global citizens" who continually realize that the similarities between people of different backgrounds, faiths, identities, and skin tones far outweigh the differences. I stand ten toes down on the belief that certain life lessons can only be learned through travel and by being in community with people unlike you; further, these lessons can only be fully understood by summoning the courage to step outside your comfort zone and crossing the mental "borders" of fear. Fear of failure, fear of the unknown, and, notably here, the fear of "putting ourselves out there" when there's always a possibility of something going wrong.

On a deeper level, I feel it's natural to be fearful of love after we've already been heartbroken, in the same way it's natural to want to avoid anything that caused us pain before. However, do we subconsciously let "outside noise"—depressing headlines filled with political turmoil, virus fears, and travel warnings—destroy our personal relationships? I believe *Love in the Time of Hate* does a beautiful job of addressing this, and I feel blessed to see it represent a modern-day maneuvering of the Game of Life—filled with slippery chutes, lengthy ladders, taboo, trivial romantic pursuits, and very few clues on how to prevent the "game of love" from becoming an unstable Jenga tower.

Susana's chronicle is more than a story for the multiculturally conscious; it's also for those who appreciate narratives written from the heart: pure, unplanned, and poetic. It's especially for those who pay a little more attention to international headlines or are curious about the modern-day barriers that infiltrate classic love stories.

FOREWORD

For the Spanglish speakers, Francophiles, Duolingo-downloaders, and anyone with the bravery to journey into new relational, professional, or geographical territory—we see you, we're with ya, and we hope you enjoy this book!

Anastascia Duchesse

Preface

I first heard of the term "romantic love" in academia during my second year of sociological studies. Sociologists gather information through surveys, data collection, and observation, but it's a bit more complicated when you're both the scientist and the case study. In that instance, you're the participant and observer. One of the most difficult tasks for any scientist is to be completely objective, and when you're in love, objectivity disappears and bias sets in.

The object of your affection is the most beautiful, most handsome, most talented, most funny, most loving person you know. They can do nothing wrong. You constantly think about that person; you want to be with them all the time; there's almost an insatiable desire for that person. The object of your desire can be a source of inspiration, increasing your confidence and motivating you to do bigger and better things, to be a better human, and to see the world differently. The sky can be falling, yet when you're in love, all is right with the world.

What's so wonderful about romantic love? Everything! The first coffee date, the first hike, the first movie, the first dance, and ah yes, that first kiss, which can make or break a relationship. So, if our love interest is the be-all end-all, why do so many people fall out of love? Among many reasons, there's a lack of commitment, poor communication, and unrealistic expectations, but more importantly, in my opinion, it is that the novelty wears off. All those firsts become fourths, fifths, and sixths.

It's not very romantic to speak about love in scientific terms, but if we talk about it in layman's terms, it's important to remember all the reasons we fell in love in the first place and to do our best to continue being that person, if not a better version. When courting, did you dress nice for that special someone? Did you ever write them a love letter? Did you sing to them? Dedicate a song? Did you share an ice cream? Did you ask her to dance? Did you send a text telling him or her how much you miss them?

When looking for love, we're searching for that one person who is going to be all that we want them to be for us. We need to remember that we have to be that person for them too. *Love in the Time of Hate* documents the thoughts, lives, and actions of two people in love while living almost unfazed in a world dominated by chaos, confusion, and hate.

Chapter 1

Romantic Love
Amor romántico

TUESDAY, OCTOBER 1, 2024
THE NEW YORK TIMES

3 Children Injured, One Seriously, in Zurich Stabbing Attack
By Amelia Nierenberg
Pez Coastal Kitchen, Pasadena

I had another episode this weekend, and I asked for some alone time. I know this is difficult for you, but you're always very respectful of my time and space. I still had reservations about seeing you this week because the pain I experience with you is different. You knew I didn't want to see you, so you planned an extra special outing.

You chose a Euro-Asian fusion *resto*; you ordered a cocktail for you and a glass of white wine for me, and I blocked the hurt I felt to shield you from my pain. I didn't hide it well, and you scrambled to take out a gift you had for me. It was a book from

1

a conversation we had the previous night, and you had already marked a page with a relevant quote.

"Fighting is the art of expressing the human body honestly"
—Bruce Lee

The thoughtful gesture was enough to help me ease into the moment. I don't remember much of what was said over those two and a half hours, but I do remember how much you made me laugh when I didn't feel like smiling.

WEDNESDAY, OCTOBER 2, 2024
THE NEW YORK TIMES

Dozens Die After Smugglers Force Them Off Ships Into Open Waters
By Amelia Nierenberg
King Taco, Pasadena

We arrived at a café late this afternoon and found it closed. The disappointment on your face was apparent, and I quickly suggested the taco place a few feet away. Your eyes glanced over at mine, and your lips parted. The puzzled look on your face perplexed me, but when you asked, "You'd eat tacos with me?," I understood.

We'd known each other for almost two years and that remark made me feel like you didn't know me at all. It was partly my fault. The persona I'd been assembling through my wardrobe, personal interests, and formal demeanor made me come across as proper and perhaps stuffy. You'd never seen me eat a burger, wear a pair of jeans, or seen my lips void of rouge.

If my appearance gave you that impression, you were partly right. However, in my defense, if you've never seen me eat a burger, it's because I make every effort to take care of myself. Wearing jeans after the age of forty, in my opinion, is a fashion faux pas that can be easily remedied by any number of flattering options. And the lip lacquer is to look lovely for you.

I was curious to see what you'd order, and you brought over two three-taco plates; asada, al pastor, and carnitas. One with no toppings and the other with everything, and you asked me to choose. I realized I wasn't the only one testing. I chose the works and generously poured the green sauce over them. Again, my choice surprised you.

Halfway through the second taco, I felt the perspiration begin to pierce through my skin, and my lips burned like the color painted on them. You saw my discomfort and were baffled by my taco selection, but is there any other way to eat a taco?

The quick workday lunch allowed us to continue our conversation in your car. You opened a box of sweet breath mints to offset the jalapeño, onion, and cilantro flavors, and I happily took two. I pulled out my phone to share a *Pepito*[1] joke I had seen on social media that reminded me a lot of you. *Chiste de Pepito y Jaimito—Tenerlo Todo* [Pepito and Jaimito Joke—"Have It All"].

You watched and listened intently, and when finished, you burst into laughter. Your body shook, and your hands switched from your face to your tummy to your face again. The *chiste* had resonated with you more than I thought it would. I was happy you laughed as much as you made me laugh yesterday.

Sweetheart, you've often told me you love to hear me laugh, but what I've never told you is how much I enjoy making you laugh. When something I've said or done triggers your laugh for days, I know I've hit a home run. Go Dodgers!

THURSDAY, OCTOBER 3, 2024
THE NEW YORK TIMES

Israeli planes target Nasrallah's likely successor with huge strikes near Beirut.
By Ronen Bergman; Ephrat Livni

---

1. Little Johnny jokes are about a little boy who innocently poses questions and makes embarrassing statements. There are many joke characters like Little Johnny around the world and in Mexico, it's Pepito. Wikipedia, "Little Johnny."

Text: *¡Un beso muy efímero a esos labios tan lindos y esa mujer tan preciosa!* [A very fleeting kiss on those pretty lips of that beautiful woman!]

FRIDAY, OCTOBER 4, 2024
THE NEW YORK TIMES

At Least 70 People Dead in Gang Attack in Haiti
By Frances Robles
Vallarta Supermarkets, Pasadena

It's all in the details they say, and you excel continually in this category.

Text: *¿Popeye o Energético?*
My response: What?!

I wasn't expecting to see you this afternoon, but there you were with *dos jugos naturales* for me to choose from. More than the kind gesture, you remembered what time my piano lesson ended, and you waited patiently for me to come out for my surprise. A welcome gift for someone who enjoys your warm embrace and beautiful smile.

SATURDAY, OCTOBER 5, 2024
THE NEW YORK TIMES

Widow of Man Killed in July Attack on Trump Returns for Rally
By Charles Homans
Starbucks Midnight Run, Pasadena

You called me yesterday late into the evening hours because you wanted to see me one more time before the end of the day. I was tired and didn't feel well, but you persuaded me with a promise of *un beso muy tierno* and a cup of hot mint tea.

We cruised; you held me like you never wanted to let me go and told me stories of your youth until my tummy settled. You didn't forget the kiss. You gazed deeply into my eyes, held me to keep me warm, kissed my hand, and caressed my cheek. You kissed my soul before your lips ever touched mine.

The link to Louis Armstrong's *"La Vie en Rose"* appeared in a text from you to me this afternoon. It triggered our continued conversation of the perfect slow dance tune. There's something very intimate about this ritual of affection that begins with the choreographed shuffling of the feet below and ends with the choreographed brushes of the cheeks above.

SUNDAY, OCTOBER 6, 2024
THE NEW YORK TIMES

Anger and Pain Permeate Observances a Year After Hamas Attack
Millennium Biltmore Hotel, Los Angeles 12:04 a.m.

We sat there amongst columns, arches, and chandeliers of the Gilded Age and two beautifully prepared drinks. You ordered a Rye Manhattan for you and a Sidecar for me. My eyes followed the elegant martini glass from its round base, long delicate stem, bright orange liquid, sugar-covered rim, and perfect orange slice garnish. For a moment, I was transported to 1920s Paris, but there was something on your mind.

It wasn't long before your smiling eyes turned sad, and you asked me where you stood in my life and what I thought of you as a person. You'd taken note of how well I've spoken of others, yet you've never heard me utter a single word about you. In contrast, you've taken every opportunity to tell me why I'm so special to you in your life.

And so, I tell you that you are an incredibly beautiful and kind human being. I've never met anyone like you, and the thought of not having shared more years of my life with you pains me. You find beauty in everything, your face doesn't know the lines of a frown, and your laughter has poured more from your lips than tears from your eyes. If I haven't been able to tell you this before, it's because you're more to me than adjectives on a résumé.

You're my sunshine on a cold winter's day, my calm in the face of a storm, and my solid foundation when the earth trembles.

I can only hope that I am at least half to you of all that you are to me.

Incoming call: 3:06 p.m.

You leave me speechless when you call me to say that you just want to hear my voice. I almost never know what to say; nevertheless, an hour later feels like only five minutes have passed. We talk about the books you've read, politics, religion, nutrition, fitness, and even fashion. My strong opinions never seem to faze you, and your passion for the moon, the stars, and outer space have a way of inciting my curiosity.

Our intense conversations often culminate in the solving of world hunger and achieving world peace.

Espero con muchas ansias our next phone date.

MONDAY, OCTOBER 7, 2024
THE NEW YORK TIMES

In a World Changed by Oct. 7, Hatred Is Winning
By Roger Cohen
L'moon Creamery, Pasadena

You wake up every morning when the first rays of sunlight hit your face, and your first thought is to wish me a wonderful day.

Text: GM sweetheart! Have a wonderful start and a beautiful day.

I did have a wonderful day, but it was the late afternoon that I looked forward to the most. This p.m.'s escapade, a loose-leaf tea dessert shop with a French flair. Its jazz playlist added an air of sophistication to this otherwise casual hangout. You ordered a Thai tea soft serve and a decadent chocolate chip walnut cookie, and we took a seat at the outdoor bench.

We laughed and giggled about nonsense as you stole pecks from me between sugary bites. Your salt-and-pepper coif was a sharp contrast to your childlike enthusiasm for your date. Your giddy demeanor reminded me of a third grader's infatuation for his grade schoolteacher. I imagined us as wide-eyed kids with our legs hanging and swinging over that very bench. I could almost hear you sighing, "Oh, Ms. Crabtree,[2] I have something heavy on my heart . . ." And my response, "Oh my Chubsy Wubsy . . ."

TUESDAY, OCTOBER 8, 2024
THE NEW YORK TIMES

A Cartel Double-Cross Turns a Mexican State Into a War Zone
By Natalie Kitroeff; Paulina Villegas
Rose Bowl, Pasadena

I didn't see you today, but you held my hand the entire way on my evening hike. You called as I took my first steps up the hill and remarked that it would be dark before I finished. Our conversation was a kaleidoscope of topics; we talked about everything and nothing at the same time. The *tête-à-tête* wasn't important to you; of greater concern to you was my safety.

The ever-evolving dialogue was dotted with intermittent safety checks: Are there more people walking with you? Are you wearing a headlamp? Are you nearing your car? The sun turned in, the moon arose, and you remained with me until my safe return.

WEDNESDAY, OCTOBER 9, 2024
THE LOS ANGELES TIMES

Anti-Asian slurs scrawled on "Dave Min for Congress" signs in Huntington Beach; suspect arrested
By Clara Harter

---

2. The name of the character who played the schoolteacher in the *Our Gang* children's comedies. Wikipedia, "June Marlowe."

Rose Bowl, Pasadena

We met at the Bowl, but we didn't get much walking done. We kissed and giggled in the parking lot, like two teens behind the bleachers after a football game. You said something that resonated with me: "We kissed before we ever hugged." It took me a sec to understand what you meant, and then I realized I had a similar thought a few weeks ago. There's something about a hug that speaks volumes more than a kiss.

You listed your favorite hugs: the one on Green Street after the soft serve ice cream, the one on Lincoln Avenue after a lengthy absence, and your favorite, the summit of Angels Flight Railway in Downtown Los Angeles at midnight because everything about it was perfect.

I don't have a favorite hug, but I do remember noticing the shift in how those hugs felt from being merely physical to becoming emotional. They run deeper. Now I want to be held longer and closer. I want to listen to the sound of your breath and be enveloped in the aroma of your shirt. I can't always guess your thoughts, but judging from the intensity of your embrace, I dare to say you feel the same.

THURSDAY, OCTOBER 10, 2024
THE LOS ANGELES TIMES

Sea lion dies after being shot in Orange County. Officials offer $20,000 reward.
By Nathan Solis
Boba ChaCha, Pasadena

No two days with you are the same. We both love surprises. I fondly remember the evening I arrived at our dinner date in a strapless summer dress. Like Richard Gere when he sees Ms. Vivian at the hotel lounge in an elegant black cocktail dress, you too stood still, smiled, and stared. And like Ms. Vivian, I made the first move and walked over to you. You didn't know whether to hug me or kiss me, but you reached out to me and held me nervously as if I would break. As we stood there and reveled in one another's presence, the rush to make it to dinner on time was no longer a priority.

There would be no dinner date this evening, but you surprised me with a quick midday visit and a large cold boba tea. The flavorful tapioca pearls and lightly flavored beverage were a welcome respite for a warm California autumn day. It came with a couple of large side orders of savory kisses and sweet hugs.

MONDAY, OCTOBER 14, 2024
THE LOS ANGELES TIMES

Deadly cartel power struggle shuts down entire Mexican city
By Patrick J. McDonnell
Castaway, Burbank

Text: GM and thank you so much.
Response: What are you thankful for?
Text: For you

You whisked me away to a place aptly named for its secluded location. A spot high above the hills with awe-inspiring panoramic views of the Los Angeles skyline, and yet we only had eyes for each other. If it had been a staring contest, I would have lost.

It is something about the way you look at me that causes me to drop my gaze, and curiously enough, you always keep your eyes on me. You don't just look at me, nor stare, but you speak to my soul, tug at my heart, and arouse in me a plethora of emotions.

You wore a suit today, and you know how much I love that. You always put in extra effort to look nice for me, and I appreciate that deeply. I couldn't stop looking at your jet-black blazer, its sharp, elegant lines, and sleek out-breast pocket. I reached over the table to remove a piece of lint resting near your left chest and *voila*, you were perfect.

You ordered a cocktail for you and a Sidecar for me. My eyes scrambled to find yours to tell you that I couldn't drink during work hours, but you insisted. Your rationale? You want me to sample Sidecars all over the world. I waved the checkered flag, and the Sidecar revved its engine. I was no match for the delicate coupe, asymmetrical sugarcoating, and perfectly round dried citrus garnish. The dehydrated orange slice floated effortlessly in the mixture as if basking in the noonday sun. By the time the Sidecar crossed the finish line, I too relished in the sun-drenched afternoon. Cheers!

TUESDAY, OCTOBER 15, 2024
PASADENA STAR-NEWS

Israel says 4 soldiers were killed by Hezbollah drone
By Wafaa Shurafa; Samy Magdy; THE ASSOCIATED PRESS

Thinking of you.

We didn't see each other today, and on days like this, you ask me if I think of you; I do, perhaps not as often as you say you think of me, but I do have many beautiful memories of us that surface. Those recollections bring me joy, laughter, and even daydreams. When I write, I think about how much you like to read; when I hear a romantic melody, I daydream of that elusive slow dance with you, and when I drive past Vallarta Supermarkets,[3] I remember the time you almost kissed me.

It was a cold evening, and you treated me to my favorite winter weather drink, champurrado. The warm, thick Mexican beverage is the perfect chocolate-based *atole*. It had been a long day, and I welcomed the invitation to sit and sip the hot, cozy liquid comfort in a paper cup. We sat at the tables inside the grocery store sandwiched between the ceviche and *chicharrones*. When we finished, you walked me to my car, and I felt your energy as you faced me to say goodbye, but there would be no first kiss. Instead, I received a kiss on my cheek, you looked at me with those bashful eyes, and we said *buenas noches*.

3. American supermarket chain founded in 1985 and concentrated mostly in Southern California. Wikipedia, "Vallarta Supermarkets."

WEDNESDAY, OCTOBER 16, 2024
PASADENA STAR-NEWS

Man Fatally Stabs Father
By Ruby Gonzales
Total Wine & More, Pasadena
Starbucks, Pasadena

This was the first time in our six-month courtship that we did something mundane. I felt guilty asking you to help me run errands, but I had to put an auction item together for charity that was due the next morning.

The scavenger hunt for my taste-of-Guatemala basket began right after work. We stopped at a local alcoholic beverage shop that carried international spirits and world market goods. We trekked past France, through Spain, over Portugal, and crossed the Atlantic to Central America. It was the Mesoamerican sugarcane-based rum we were after, and the selection didn't disappoint.

We could almost smell the sweet, fruity aroma and taste the dark, caramelized flavor of the auburn liquid courage. The basket quickly became booze heavy, so we continued our search for products in the evergreen coffee plantations of Guatemala's highlands and added a pound of freshly ground java. No coffee compares to beans cultivated in volcanic soil from the land of eternal spring. I loved that you couldn't help but take a long whiff and relish in the scent of the chocolate, nutty medium roast.

Jet-lagged and weary, we sat in your car, caressing each other's faces when you paused for a moment to tell me how much fun we have together. I couldn't agree more.

THURSDAY, OCTOBER 17, 2024
THE LOS ANGELES TIMES

Combs' UCLA arrest in 2015 detailed; Music mogul allegedly put a football program employee in headlock and choked an intern.
By Richard Winton and Hannah Fry

Pasadena Hilton 7:30 a.m.

It was showtime. The fundraising event we worked so hard for had arrived. The tables were set, the auction items were in place, and the emcee had the crowd's attention. As we sat there enjoying the program, you casually faced me and wished me a happy anniversary. I was taken aback by your romantic remark. Unable to respond, I simply looked at you and smiled. You continued by saying that it was almost two years to the day that we first met at that exact event. I couldn't believe you remembered.

I shouldn't have been surprised you recalled that day. You told me on more than one occasion that you fell in love with me the moment you saw me. The French have a phrase for it, *coup de foudre*. The term literally translates to "bolt of lightning." It accurately describes a sudden feeling of love that comes over the person. It took me a little bit longer, about a year and a half, to be exact. It's these demonstrations of affection, however, that cause me to fall in love with you more and more each day.

Think Prime Steak House, Rancho Palos Verdes, 7:30 p.m.

There's something about the way you make me feel that makes me want to look beautiful for you every day. You demonstrate a sincere appreciation for my sense of style, and I enjoy your reaction when you see me wearing something new. This evening, I wore an asymmetrical winter-white jumpsuit, and I wrapped myself in a matching belted coat. You picked me up for our short road trip to San Pedro. I hadn't been there in more than twenty years, so I was looking forward to our little venture. We stopped for a light dinner on our way to our destination.

You stepped out of the car to open the door for me, but you had an ulterior motive: to get a better look at my ensemble. You helped me out of the car, and we stood there on the sidewalk parallel to the busy boulevard facing one another. You untied my belt, unraveled my coat, and I could tell by your subtle smile and sparkle in your eyes that you loved the look. You gave me a soft kiss, held me in your arms for a few moments, took me by the hand, and walked me in.

We were warmly greeted and escorted to our booth by the chef himself. I detected a French accent, and normally, I would have struck up a conversation, but this was our time, and I wanted to spend every second of it with you. The sweet French accent paired well with the savory voice of the country music singer performing just a few feet away. We sat in a cushioned half-moon, tall back booth that offered just enough privacy with a grand view of the establishment, and a direct line of sound to the performer. He had a lovely voice with a soft Southern drawl. Every love song he sang seemed like it was written for us. My eyes shied away from yours every time he uttered the word "love," and as always, you kept your eyes on me. You even began singing along with the playlist that must have been taken straight out of your 1980s mixed cassette tapes.

You ordered a Rye Manhattan for you, and a Sidecar for me; we shared a shrimp appetizer and an exceptionally well-prepared seafood dish. You sliced the jumbo shrimp into bite-sized pieces, squeezed a slice of lemon over them, dipped them in the sauce, and carefully fed me each morsel. You even placed your hand beneath my mouth to prevent anything from falling on my suit.

We chatted, enjoyed each other's company, and laughed like two mischievous teens in detention hall. I've never seen you so joyful, and I was happy I felt the same way. Who knew I would find my three greatest loves in a steak house in Rancho Palos Verdes, a taste of French culture, live country music, and you.

FRIDAY, OCTOBER 18, 2024
THE LOS ANGELES TIMES

Former Olympian ran drug empire, ordered murders, feds allege
By Noah Goldberg
Pacific Diner, San Pedro
Korean Friendship Bell, San Pedro
22nd St. Landing Seafood Grill & Bar, San Pedro

You took me to a popular breakfast eatery that opened the same year I was born. I was immediately transported back to my childhood of comfort food meals with my parents, unlimited coffee refills, and clanking ceramic dishes. Oh, how I miss places like this. White toast with butter and strawberry jam, pork chops, biscuits and gravy, homestyle potatoes and eggs sunny-side up, oh my! Like the good kids we were raised to be, we cleaned our plates and left to enjoy the rest of our day.

You next drove me to a park on a bluff overlooking the vast Pacific Ocean. There, in the middle of the green, under the sun, surrounded by the blue, sat an ornate, Asian-inspired belfry. It took me a moment to realize you brought me to a Korean War memorial. I was so moved by your thoughtfulness that I couldn't find the words to tell you how special this visit was for me.

I've been working for three years with a committee to place a monument in remembrance of the Korean War conflict at Pasadena's Memorial Park. It's truly been a labor of love to form the committee, find support, and create something that pays homage to those who paid the ultimate price for the freedoms we enjoy today.

The bell may have been created from seventeen tons of copper and tin, with gold, nickel, and lead, but its elegant shape and beautifully carved exterior gave it the feathery appearance of a Christmas tree ornament hung on a limb. The bell was presented by the South Korean government to the United States to celebrate the 1976 US bicentennial and as a symbol of friendship between the two countries.

You filled my heart with love and my soul with peace, but you felt compelled to fill my tummy at a San Pedro staple. The waterfront restaurant came with a complete view of the Cabrillo Marina, which featured meandering seagulls, an array of small boats and yachts, and what I thought was the SS Minnow[4] leaving the harbor. We sat alongside the floor-to-ceiling windows of this nautical gem and watched the sun's rays glisten over the water. You ordered the

---

4. The SS Minnow is the fictional charter boat from the 1960s television show "Gilligan's Island." Wikipedia, "Gilligan's Island."

catch of the day, and as tasty as it was, we were unhurried to finish. I don't think either of us wanted this day to end.

TUESDAY, OCTOBER 22, 2024
THE LOS ANGELES TIMES

Suspect crashes into Fresno home during pursuit; 2 sisters killed
By Clara Harter
Élephante, Santa Monica
Temescal Canyon Falls, Pacific Palisades

The eight hours we spent together today felt like five minutes. You picked me up, and we headed west. The morning traffic was heavy, but I looked forward to some alone time with you, even if it meant sitting in a car. One of my favorite songs, Kaoma's, "Lambada" was on your playlist. A fitting soundtrack for our lunch date. We arrived at the Italian-inspired *ristorante* overlooking what would be the Mediterranean Sea and took a spot on the balcony at a table for two. We'd spoken all weekend by phone, and suddenly, neither of us had a thing to say, and we didn't need to. I could tell by your smiling eyes that you had something on your mind, but I left it up to you to tell me whenever you were ready to share.

I couldn't help but admire your handpicked stitched blazer. A sewing technique rarely used these days, found only in more refined pieces, and a remnant of a time when dressing up for a meal was considered the norm. As we sat there drowning in an ocean of T-shirts and flip-flops, you made sure I had something nice to appreciate, and I can't tell you how much I enjoyed the view.

We eventually struck up a conversation about *Love in the Time of Cholera* and *One Hundred Years of Solitude*. It wasn't the first time we discussed Gabriel García Márquez, and I am sure it will not be the last. We conversed about flowery descriptive language and how writers sometimes overdo it. I love to use flowery language myself, mostly because I want to remember as many details as I can about the special moments in my life.

You ordered a caprese salad, seared scallops, and a creamy pasta dish. You made a comment about the pasta's salty content, and although you were right, it had a surprisingly different effect on me. Its salinity swept me into a backward current to a place in time when I sat at a bistro on the Mediterranean Sea overlooking the Cote d'Azur. Its astonishing beauty is one of the few places in the world where reality is more exquisite than the postcard. I didn't want our lunch date to end, but you had other plans for us, or at least I thought you did. When the elevator doors closed, I realized you couldn't wait to kiss me. Your *beso* came straight out of a telenovela's climax when the *protagonista* finally embraces his love interest, and she melts in his arms.

We hopped on the California 1, hung a right on Sunset, and found ourselves in Temescal Canyon. We changed our shoes; you put on your Steve Irwin shirt; we grabbed a bottle of water and started down the oak-tree-lined path. It was our first hike together. We first discussed hiking about two years ago at our first coffee meeting. I had recently published a book about hiking, and you wanted to learn all about it, or me, as you later confessed.

We sat at the sidewalk café sipping tea, exchanging ideas, and talking about the granddaddy of all hikes, the Camino de Santiago. I remember that day like it was yesterday. You've had that same beautiful smile, contagious laugh, and love of life since the moment we met.

We didn't quite finish our hike this afternoon. The plan to reach the waterfall was disrupted by your repeated acts of affection. I didn't mind you stopping every few feet for a kiss or warm embrace. On the contrary, I would have been disappointed if you hadn't.

Chapter 2

The Love Letter
La carta de amor

THURSDAY, OCTOBER 24, 2024
THE LOS ANGELES TIMES

UCLA surveys say hate persists on 2 sides
By Jaweed Kaleem
Noor, Pasadena

Tonight's gala was a special occasion we both looked forward to. It was our first formal together, and you were excited to be my plus-one. My enthusiasm for the event deteriorated after a canceled hair appointment, two wardrobe failures, and a damaged car door. We met in the parking garage, and I saw the genuine look of concern on your face. All I could verbalize was to ask you to please take me to my office. I had supplies in my desk drawer that would allow me to at least address the wardrobe issue.

    More than half a dozen garment adhesives later, both my bulging side zipper and cleavage were secure. I still didn't feel well, but you have all the love and patience of a saint. You lowered your voice, held my hand, and offered to hold my belongings. You couldn't have been more of a gentleman in your conduct and appearance.

You were impeccably dressed in a modern black tuxedo with a satin lapel, silver and black onyx studs with matching cuff links, a bow tie, and a pair of perfectly polished patent leather Oxfords. All I wanted to do was to calm down enough to tell you how handsome you looked and how touched I was by your efforts to look nice for me. I'd almost managed to ruin my efforts to do the same for you.

At the pre-event mixer, we reconnected with friends, had a glass of Sauvignon Blanc, and posed for pictures. The start of our evening hadn't gone as planned, but I was grateful by the way you handled the situation with your cool demeanor and sense of maturity.

At long last, I turned to tell you how handsome you looked; your perfect response, "You're gorgeous." My eyes briefly met yours, we smiled, and I bashfully looked away. We sat with friends, made new ones, joined hands to say grace, and talked about religion, work, and politics. All taboo subjects, but by the eve's end, we all felt more connected than we were when we first walked in.

FRIDAY, OCTOBER 25, 2024
THE LOS ANGELES TIMES

Dark-web dealer of drugs led a lavish lifestyle; Two face federal sentencing for selling fentanyl-laced pills, cocaine on internet.
By Jireh Deng
Arroyo Vista Inn, South Pasadena

As if you hadn't already thought of every detail to make the evening special, you reserved a charming bedroom suite. The guest house and tearoom were well hidden in plain view on a solitary hill. It wasn't the first time you'd brought me to this charming getaway; however, I'm appreciative that your unexpected sojourns always occur on days when I need them most.

My stomach woke up before I did, and I couldn't wait for breakfast. You changed into your favorite Steve Irwin button shirt, and I put on my embroidered silk, floor-length gown with a tail and wrapped myself in a coat. I hadn't packed a change of clothes, though, dating you, I should always be prepared for anything.

We sat at a table for two by the window overlooking the patio, and you ordered two eggs over easy, toast with grape jelly, a cup of coffee, and a glass of warm frothy milk for two. I felt uncomfortably overdressed, but your smile afforded me the sense of peace I needed, and within minutes, we found ourselves laughing.

I finally told you about how your shirt reminded me of the late zoologist Steve Irwin and how you channeled him while hiking the other day. On our trek, you went on about the sounds and rituals of the local doves and owls, and I commented on how entertaining that was.

My attention momentarily shifted to the printed textile in front of me. I couldn't help but admire and run my fingers over the French-inspired table covering, but by your quizzical expression, I could tell that you had no idea why I'd been distracted and so taken by it.

I wish there was a way to place you in my memories to share my experiences with you. The paprika-tinted walls and bright floral patterns of the tablecloth brought back cherished souvenirs of weekly strolls down the sun-drenched isles of Le Grand Marché in Aix-en-Provence. Bouquets of fragrant flowers, perfectly rounded truckles and orbs of cheese, the town's sweet herbal lavender scent that permeated throughout, and bolts of exquisitely printed colorful fabrics.

Provence was my home before my eyes ever saw it, and my heart was yours before we ever met.

SATURDAY, OCTOBER 26, 2024
THE LOS ANGELES TIMES

Rapper arrested in plot to slay rival in 2022; Officials say Lil Durk's hit team killed target's cousin in an ambush near Beverly Center.

Love in the Time of Hate

By Matthew Ormseth; Karen Garcia
Trattoria Daly, Lincoln Heights

I surprised you with an afternoon visit, and you surprised me with a romantic dinner. You chose a trattoria that you'd been wanting to take me to for some time. The small, charming establishment offered several seating options. The single outdoor bistro table, although *al fresco* didn't offer any privacy. The large dining area was too brightly lit, and the smaller side room was narrow and cramped. Goldilocks finally found the chair that suited her best in the back patio area. Dimly lit, intimate, yet spacious, and secluded. We sat down just as the gardener finished tending to his oak barrel garden beds. His leafy greens couldn't have been happier than if they had been grown in Liguria, Italy. You ordered red wine, a medium rare steak, and a freshly picked caprese salad.

It was game two of the Dodgers in the World Series, and Lincoln Heights was at the epicenter. LAPD choppers thundered overhead, sirens blared below, cars raced down North Broadway, and as if right on queue, Andrea Bocelli's "*Por ti Volaré*" played in the background.

This evening's topic of discussion, our first kiss. It wasn't the first time we'd talked about it, but the *Lady and the Tramp* atmosphere allowed for a better analysis of our initial encounter.

It was a weeknight, and you asked me to go out for drinks. I accepted, but the drink date developed into a drawn-out drive. Car sickness set in, and I asked you to please stop the car. You parked on the side of the road; we spoke for a few minutes, and you went for it. I learned a lot about you from that first smooch. It was something that you had given thought to for a while; it took a lot of courage on your part to risk a well-established relationship and of most interest to me was that you were a little out of practice. I found the latter quite endearing, but we hadn't discussed this final detail until this evening.

We couldn't help but laugh at the awkwardness of that *primer beso*, and when a couple walked in on us laughing, they referred to us as *los enamorados*. I wonder what they would have said if they would have walked in on us kissing.

MONDAY, OCTOBER 28, 2024
THE NEW YORK TIMES

Man Who Made Violent Threats Skirted Arrest and Then Shot a Neighbor
By Amanda Holpuch; Hank Sanders
L'moon Creamery, Pasadena

Text: I want to thank you! I'll tell you why later, okay, baby?

Each morning for more than two decades, I've sat myself down for a complete breakfast with eggs, toast, avocado, fruit, yogurt, and coffee. It is quality time that I dedicate to myself, and I often share this basic ritual with others in hopes that they, too, will do the same. You may be the first who has taken my advice to heart.

Today, you thanked me for reminding you of how important it is to sit for a meal, use real dinnerware, and more importantly, to share that quality time with family. You've taught me something equally valuable, that love and romance still exist. I asked you once how it is that you are so romantic, and you responded that I was the reason. And you are my reason for showing you love in return.

THURSDAY, OCTOBER 31, 2024
THE NEW YORK TIMES

Librarians Face a Crisis of Violence and Abuse
By Christina Caron
Alice's Dog Park, Pasadena

Text: Your chariot awaits my Lady

I sent you a picture of my egg-less breakfast, and you adjusted your schedule to bring me a dozen. You said you wanted to make sure your baby had her eggs. I never imagined my heart would go pitter-patter over groceries, but I was genuinely moved by your thoughtfulness.

You drove us to a park where you pulled out our favorite serape and spread it between the gopher mounds on a patch of green under the shade of two trees. We sat down, and a ground squirrel popped his head out to greet us. You looked at me *con esos ojos de enamorado*, you pressed your lips against mine, and a little bit of sadness fell over me. I thought about the kisses we've worked on for months to perfect, and I wondered if you'd be giving them to someone else one day?

I scrambled to erase the thought from my mind and moved on to talk about our love language bucket list.

- Romantic movie and popcorn

- Slow dance

- *Mariachi* serenade

And the most recently added, the love letter. It was something you'd thought about as well, but you hadn't put pen to paper, just fingertips to screen when texting.

I grew up with pen pals, and I loved the entire process of writing, receiving, and mailing a note. But how could I ask you to do something that I hadn't done myself for you?

Mi Querido,

I don't remember ever having penned a letter of love to someone. In truth, I am sure I have not. I couldn't have understood in my younger years the intricacy of this intense emotion that can be conveyed through a simple glance, a subtle touch, or a gentle smile. A power so great that it forces my eyes to shy away, my fingers to reach out, and my lips to smile.

As a child, I dreamt of my principe azul. As imaginative as I was, I could never piece together the features of his face, but I knew that he would choose me for that special dance.

You taught me that romance is more than a waltz; it's making me a peanut butter and jelly sandwich for lunch, sending me the lyrics to a song that says everything you feel in your heart, and having the patience for the one you love to finally love you back.

I could never have imagined a face more beautiful than yours. One whose eyes light up when they see mine, whose facial lines deepen when they smile at me, and whose lips still quiver when they speak to me.

You made my fairy tale of white chariots, grand balls, and castles up on a hill a reality.

Lo quiero con todo mi corazón,
Your Lady

SATURDAY, NOVEMBER 2, 2024

Omni Hotel, Los Angeles

We both had evening engagements, so when we finished, we met somewhere in the middle. The signs of fall were all around us, the freshly fallen rain, the mirror pools on the ground, and the crisp outdoor temps. The elements made the trench coat you wore even more stylish. I loved the textured polka-dot tie you chose for your ensemble; I couldn't help but admire it and run my fingers over it.

We stepped into the lobby of the hotel, and memories of my teen years came flooding back. Someone was celebrating their fortieth, and the DJ must have flown in on a DeLorean. He mixed every popular nineties song, but when he played "Atomic Dog," it took every ounce of willpower I had to not crash the party. That tune played at each of my high school dances, and I freestyled to it every time.

You began moving to the song, and you would have crashed the party with me just so I could relive a few moments of my gym homecoming years.

You ordered two cocktails and a Thai chicken dish to share. Everything always tastes better with you. We talked about politics, and as sensitive as that topic is for me, it always seems to creep into our conversation.

The damp outdoor patio was visible through the floor-to-ceiling raindrop-splattered windows. You couldn't help but look outside. I could tell that every part of you wanted to hold and kiss me under the rain just as much as I wanted to shake my tush on that dance floor. I gave in, and we stepped out into the California deluge. There was no precipitation, only puddles, but you pulled me towards you at the earliest opportunity. You make me feel tiny when you wrap your hands around my waist, and I love it. You held me, kissed me, and caressed my face in every nook of that courtyard terrace.

Like in the well-known fairy tale, the clock struck midnight, I ran down the slippery stairs, I got into my pumpkin, and although I didn't lose my shoe, a part of me stayed behind.

MONDAY, NOVEMBER 4, 2024
THE LOS ANGELES TIMES

Northern California man arrested after father's body is found inside a dumpster
By Grace Toohey
Election Day Eve

TUESDAY, NOVEMBER 5, 2024
PASADENA STAR-NEWS

SoCal law enforcement agencies prepare for potential election-related protests, upheaval
By Nathanial Percy
Hi-Life Burgers, South Pasadena
Central Park, Pasadena

Yesterday evening, you gave me the most wonderful kiss, which ended with a one-sided screaming match. It was election eve, and our conversation turned political. Unfortunately, after more than a decade of being on the inside track of local politics, my tolerance is dismal at best. It didn't take much to lose my temper, and I took it out on you.

I felt bad this morning, as you did, however, we both needed space.

Text: Hey, I'm having lunch delivered to you—where should they take it?

I was a little annoyed but happy to hear from you. I was already outside the building, occupied with something else, when you drove up with lunch in hand. I wanted to kiss you and give you a dirty look; I did both.

You brought me a burger and fries and a cheeseburger and onion rings from a place I frequented as a tween. The local hamburger joint was just down the street from my school, and I'd use my bus money for a coveted junior burger and happily forfeit the 1.5-mile RTD[1] ride home. The greasy minced-meat sandwich provided me with just enough fuel to make the long uphill trek.

We made a picnic out of the combos at a nearby park, where my mom used to take me. I have vivid memories of me climbing all over the funny-looking multi-trunk palm tree. I'd imagine myself standing on the main deck of a pirate ship. I couldn't quite reach the crow's nest, but I'd sit and watch the masts move in the wind as I sailed off into the sunset. We missed the setting sun by about an hour, but I enjoyed watching its rays bounce off your beautiful face.

We talked, signed a treaty of peace and amity, and you gave me a kiss that rivaled the prior evening's.

---

1. The Southern California Rapid Transit District (SCRTD), more popularly known as the as RTD, was a public transportation agency established in 1964 to serve the Greater Los Angeles area. Wikipedia, "Los Angeles County Metropolitan Transportation Authority."

FRIDAY, NOVEMBER 8, 2024
THE NEW YORK TIMES

Antisemitic Attacks Prompt Emergency Flights for Israeli Soccer Fans
By John Yoon; Christopher F. Schuetze; Jin Yu Young; Claire Moses
Altadena Crest Trail Cobb Estate Trailhead, Altadena

My piano lesson was canceled, and you seized the opportunity to take me on an improvised hike. You recently committed to a six-week fitness challenge, and I love the idea of venturing on to this new path together. The cool afternoon temperatures, accompanied by the sounds of the babbling brook and gentle filtered rays of sunlight, made for ideal wandering conditions.

In earlier hiking discussions, we discovered how differently we viewed this hobby. I saw it strictly as a physical activity, and you viewed it as a time to enjoy nature. The combination of both made this hike special.

The stream eventually sparked a water discussion that lasted most of the climb. In a clearing, you stopped to face me like you'd done many times before, but it wasn't to kiss me. Instead, you held me in your arms and told me that you didn't want me to see anyone like I see you; you didn't want me to kiss anyone like I kiss you, and you didn't want me to hug anyone like I hug you. Your impromptu speech concluded with a question that I never thought you'd ask; you wanted to know if I'd be your girlfriend.

My eyes turned towards the ground, I felt my face get warm, and my lips smile. I instantly reverted into a coy teenager being asked out for the first time. It took me a moment to reply, but I accepted, and you responded with an equally gleeful expression. We kissed. However, there was something about this mutual embrace that was different. You would later share the same thought. I'm uncertain if it was the enchantment of the forest or the magic of the spring that magnified its intensity, but it was by far our best kiss.

SATURDAY, NOVEMBER 9, 2024
THE NEW YORK TIMES

How Ukraine's Widows Are Shouldering Their Grief
By Maria Varenikova; Nicole Tung; Evelina Riabenko
All India Café, Pasadena
The Bissell House, South Pasadena

For our first boyfriend-girlfriend date, you chose the Indian sub-continent. A mélange of many different customs and traditions, and the café you selected didn't disappoint. Our charismatic young host greeted us with the wine list and *carte du jour*. His energy was contagious, and his enthusiasm for international cuisine was palpable. To accompany our host's recommendations, you made several choices that were familiar to me. I casually mentioned this eatery in a past conversation, and you made a mental note of my favorite dishes. If you wanted to impress me, you did. Your attention to detail is unparalleled, and any woman would appreciate that immensely.

In addition to the chicken tikka masala and lentil soup, you placed an order for panipuri shots and *Gulabi Farfalle*. Served on a mini-Indian street food cart, the crispy filled puffs were an explosion of spicy mint and tamarind flavors that caused our lips to pucker and our cheek muscles to contract. By contrast, the Indian-Italian fusion pasta dish was the perfect comfort food combination of flavors from the East and textures from the West.

I sat there listening to both you and the intricate subtle melodies and complex rhythms of South Asia. As beautiful as the music was, I knew it would be another slow dance miss. My disappointment was short-lived, as I was swiftly distracted by your uncanny talent to keep me entertained, albeit with an anecdote, an idea, or a joke.

You've told me on several occasions that you love to hear me laugh, and you take every opportunity to do just that. I chuckled at something you said, and your smile instantly grew bigger.

India is a destination that has eluded my travels, but the hanging Moroccan lanterns, ornate gilded mirrors, and culinary tour guide made me feel like we were somewhere in the Orient. I turned to look out the bay window, and for a moment, I expected a tuk-tuk to pass by. Like serious foodies, we enjoyed our meal, and although we waited for the motorized rickshaw, it never came. We were left to our own devices to maneuver the bustling streets of Pasadena.

Luckily, we didn't have to go far. You surprised me with a stay in a Queen Anne Victorian home. A structure built during an era when poetry was popular, love letters were left, and music was made. It was a time that was greatly influenced by the Empress of India herself, Queen Victoria. As tumultuous as the history between the two countries has been, the fruits of their mutual influence of love and romance continue to this day.

You didn't recite a poem, write a letter, or even perform a serenade; however, it was one of the most romantic evenings we've spent together.

Tea anyone?

WEDNESDAY, NOVEMBER 13, 2024
THE NEW YORK TIMES

Suicide Bomber in Brazil's Capital Rattles Nation Ahead of Global Summit
By Ana Ionova
The Comet Club, Pasadena

You asked me out for tea this afternoon, and part of me knew better, but my other half conceded. Tea for two was served in the lobby of a local hotel with a twenties vibe. I'd gotten upset with you the previous evening, and remnants of that discussion lingered in my thoughts.

You found a settee wedged between two walls, a coffee table, two chairs, and wall-to-wall windows. The conversation went well, but your behavior was off-putting, leaving me feeling empty and insecure. I mentioned it to you, and I was relieved you acknowledged my concerns. To say that relationships are difficult is an understatement but understanding what we expect from one another is a start.

Text: When my tummy butterflies run crazy circles and my intuition tells me I messed up something big time, I want to make things right, better, or make every effort to reconcile my errors. I didn't know how bad it was until I heard your voice this afternoon. No apology will be good enough. I will always treat you with respect and love. Please try to forget this faux pas of mine and any other time I have lowered your expectations of me. You bring out the best in me and I will remember. *Te quiero mucho.*

Response: I know Baby. I do appreciate you saying that, but I'm a little emotionally spent from the last two days. I'm not doing this to make you feel bad, but I need some me time. It takes me time to recover and although I looked like I was okay yesterday, I wasn't. It usually takes me a couple of days to mend, but when you offered tea, I thought it would be a nice way to calm my nerves, unfortunately it didn't work out that way. I know that you want me to be okay right away, but I don't work like that. I know you see me smile a lot, but I get sad too.

THURSDAY, NOVEMBER 14, 2024
THE NEW YORK TIMES

Lebanese Official Says Israeli Strikes Killed at Least 12 Emergency Workers
By Liam Stack; Aaron Boxerman; Euan Ward

Text: Take a look at the moon Baby.

They say that it's difficult to like something you don't understand. For some, it's math, for others, it's technology, and for me, it's the moon, the universe, and everything in between.

It was January 1986, and the world was abuzz with outer space. Even the library celebrated the previous summer reading season with a galaxy theme. By fall, every school in America was learning all about Christa McAuliffe, the high school teacher from New Hampshire, who would be the first educator in space.

I was in the fourth grade, and although I consider Mr. Harinaka one of the best teachers I've ever had, I never quite understood why he hadn't made a big deal of the Challenger launch as other teachers had. In hindsight, I'm glad he didn't. I'm not sure how my nine-year-old self would have taken seeing someone that I had gotten to know through lesson plans be killed on live television. I often wonder about those kids who did. It goes without saying that my enthusiasm for the cosmos never took off. Perhaps it will be you who will ignite that interest in me.

FRIDAY, NOVEMBER 15, 2024
LOS ANGELES TIMES

Horror as a girl's killer gets parole; Relatives demand justice in the death of another child, which remains unsolved.
By Brittny Mejia
Arroyo Terrace, Pasadena

It was an emotional week for us, and when you asked to see me this afternoon, I wanted to say no, but I couldn't do that. Even when I'm hurt, I want to be mindful of you and your feelings. I arrived at one of our meeting places, and you were waiting patiently for me. You hugged me and handed me an envelope. You saw the sadness in my eyes and asked if I was OK. I gave you the same response I had given you earlier that I was tired and added that it was difficult for me to be on point for everyone all the time. To which you responded that you wanted to make sure you were always on point for me. It meant a lot to hear you say that.

I am, like many women, the embodiment of Mary Poppins. In public, impeccably dressed, able to quickly solve any issue, and often with a good attitude and big smile, but it takes a toll.

I waited to be alone to open the envelope. Inside the gold seal was a seed card with a printed heart and a two-page handwritten letter. I hadn't read the first word, and my eyes welled up. I was moved by your efforts to put your thoughts in writing. You're always encouraging me to write, and I know you can write volumes more than me.

The card: To my girlfriend! Happy one week! *Te quiero mucho! XO*

Baby,

I love having you constantly on my mind. As I write this letter to you, there are so many things I want to share with you. I smile silly at times at thoughts of our growing list of things we want to do together. It is not silly. It is a part of our relationship that continues to grow as we do these things and find out how we both like them. I smile at the many firsts we've had together and the many to come. I smile at the thought of our first slow dance, a movie with popcorn, and our time just holding each other in our arms.

Since our first kiss, it seems that we have been almost inseparable, with very few exceptions. I seldom think of the months it took me to build up the courage to kiss you. The many times we shared a drink, a meal, a champurrado, a step closer to finally a kiss as awkward as it may have been.

Our short journey thus far is filled with so many emotions, let alone the last week since I asked you to be my Girlfriend. I believed you were my Girlfriend the moment I kissed you.

From the moment I met you, I knew and felt that I was coming toward a change in my life. A change I had not felt in some time. The way you smiled, spoke, and looked at me as we had our first coffee or tea that afternoon. I remember calling you and meeting you. I was so nervous approaching you, that's the reason I can't remember what I drank.

This was just the beginning, and I was already feeling like a teenager with a crush on the most beautiful girl on campus. I still feel that way today every time we meet.

I smile at the thought of being with you, doing the silliest things to planning with you the most serious things like your house and personal life, which I believe affect our relationship. The few things and times that our lives could have been different due to whatever reason whether it was my doing or yours. I shiver at the thought of not being with you now or ever . . .

Baby, my thoughts are always with you, and I look to the next time and moment we share a long hug, our arms wrapped, feeling the warmth of our bodies and the feelings we both share for each other.

Te quiero mucho.

Siempre pensando en ti.

Chapter 3

The Romantic Movie
La película romántica

SATURDAY, NOVEMBER 16, 2024
THE NEW YORK TIMES

China Hit Again With Fatal Violence as at Least 8 Die in Stabbing
By Claire Fu; Alan Yuhas
Huntington Health, Pasadena

I sat at the same hospital cafeteria table where you and I sat a little more than a year ago to discuss my next book project. My dad was in the hospital for the third time in two months. Thankfully, it wasn't anything serious. I couldn't say the same for my hunger pangs. I'd worked all day, the last full meal I had was before sunrise, and now dinner with Dad was canceled. As far as hospital food ratings are concerned, if this canteen could have been awarded Michelin Stars, it deserves at least one.

    Growing up, I lived around the corner from the medical center, and every now and then, my friends and I would sneak over to buy a burger or something. The prices were reasonable, and because their clientele included doctors and nurses, the quality was decent.

My fatigue and cooler temperatures prompted a craving for ravioli in marinara sauce and a cup of hot gumbo chicken soup. I settled into my chair to enjoy my bowls of comfort and to text updates to friends and family. Within minutes, you called and kept me company. When I was finished, you asked me to step outside, and there you were with a big smile, arms outstretched, ready to give me a hug. And oh boy, did I need one.

You walked towards me wearing a half-tucked Dodger jersey and matching baseball cap that partially hid your disheveled hair. You looked as if you had just walked off the set of an *Our Gang* baseball scene filming. I didn't care. I just wanted you to hug and kiss me as if I were your Ms. Crabtree. And that you did.

TUESDAY, NOVEMBER 19, 2024
PASADENA STAR-NEWS

4 stabbed in 2 unrelated incidents in Glendale
CITY NEWS SERVICE
Village French Bakery, Glendale

Tucked away in the foothills is a tiny French bakery with Main-Street USA as its backdrop, and a clock whose hands froze at the turn of the twentieth century. A remnant of an era when ladies strolled with their parasols and gentlemen tipped their hats. The vineyards and citrus orchards are long gone, but one can still enjoy a glass of wine, or a fruit-filled pastry. The early morning hour called for the latter.

The bakery display cases were filled with tartes, cookies, and *gâteauxs*. The little girl in me had her eyes fixed on every fluffy buttercream-frosting-covered pastry, but in that sense, you are more grown up than me. Your pick from today's menu: two lattes, a mini apple tart, and a ham-and-cheese croissant. And that's croissant with a French R, a velar fricative/ʁ/, as opposed to a "rolled" or "flipped." You couldn't help yourself, and you ordered a croissant with an /ʁ/.

Like seasoned Parisians we took a seat *en plein air* at a bistro table for two. I sat there studying the street canvass as I had Van Gogh's café terrace in Arles.

I remember standing in the middle of the sidewalk and staring at a scene that looked vastly different from the masterpiece. I knew it wouldn't be the same, but somehow, I expected it to arouse the same emotions the painting had evoked in me. Here I was, twenty years later, now an artist in my own right, painting a picture of this café, but unlike Van Gogh, I am a writer and a scientist who hopes to portray an objective reality, one that closely depicts this moment somewhere in time.

I could tell you were anxious by the way you surveyed the table: napkins check, utensils check, and sugar packets check. I didn't want to add to your butterflies, so I said very little and leaned over to give you a peck. It wasn't enough to calm you, but I wanted to reassure you it was OK. Your jitters shifted from your hands to your vocals, prompting you to ramble on a bit. I find it endearing that after months of seeing each other, for you, it's always our first date.

WEDNESDAY, NOVEMBER 20, 2024
THE NEW YORK TIMES

US Pauses Operations at Kyiv Embassy, Warning of "Significant Air Attack"
By Marc Santora
Go Go Sushi, Pasadena

Text: I'm close by Baby

Your message arrived at the perfect time. My tough morning called for a sympathetic ear, a handhold, and two twenty-second hugs. Not only did you deliver, but you added sashimi. I was baffled by your choice of a table for four, but when you took the seat next to mine, I realized you thought I needed a little more comforting, and you were right.

You asked me to pass the soy sauce so you could prepare your soy-wasabi concoction. The mixture appeared appetizing, so I prepared one for myself with less wasabi. We chewed edamame, sampled sashimi, and you paired them with a warm smile and sweet nothings in my ear.

As my wasabi confidence grew, I felt compelled to take another fraction of a teaspoon. On contact, the pungent spices shot through my nose like vapor rub on a sick day. I felt the heat rush through my cheeks, my eyes well up, and subsequently teardrops roll down my face. What did you do? You scooped up a small dollop of wasabi and placed it in your mouth. Your face turned red, your eyes welled up, and your nose became runny. I guess we both needed a good cry.

THURSDAY, NOVEMBER 21, 2024
THE NEW YORK TIMES

At Least 38 Killed as Gunmen Ambush Shiite Convoys in Pakistan
By Zia Ur-Rehman

Text: Daydreaming
Response: What are you daydreaming Sweetheart?
Text: Watching a full movie with you in my arms.

FRIDAY, NOVEMBER 22, 2024
LOS ANGELES TIMES

Man who told of girl's body in 1979 is shown to be her killer
By Noah Goldberg

Text: *¡Buenos días, amor, te deseo un hermoso día con mucho éxito en tu preparación para tu entrevista documental!* [Good morning, love, I wish you a beautiful day with great success in preparation for your documentary interview!]

SATURDAY, NOVEMBER 23, 2024
THE NEW YORK TIMES

Sectarian Violence Kills at Least 25 in Northwest Pakistan
By Zia Ur-Rehman
Trattoria Daly, Lincoln Heights

Text: Are you close by Baby?

We went to what is now one of our favorite spots, a neighborhood eatery with vintage appeal and a welcoming vibe. Since our last visit, temperatures dropped significantly, so outdoor seating was no longer an option. My disappointment was short-lived as our host found a table for us in the smaller dining area that offered relative privacy. Call me selfish, but on the rare occasions that we see each other, I want you all to myself.

I want to be able to look at you, hold your hand, and have a conversation with minimal distractions or interruptions. And I felt fortunate that we were able to do that this evening. I didn't see you order, but when the meal arrived, you gave me the option to choose. I forwent the omega-3 fatty acids, set my calorie-counting thoughts aside, and opted for the beef lasagna. I was no match for the multiple pasta layers, gooey mozzarella cheese, and chunks of ground beef.

We celebrated the completion of day fifteen of your six-week challenge. It never ceases to amaze me how quickly men can get in shape. I saw you earlier this evening at your book reading. It was the first time; your face appeared different to me. It was slimmer.

I wasn't sure how to feel about that because the person I was seeing wasn't the person I fell in love with. I sat there for a moment, studying your new facial features, your posture, and the way your clothing conformed to your new shape. I had the urge to sift through my photo gallery and examine before and after pictures. I didn't have time to do that, nor did I need to.

Any lingering questions I had about who this new person was dissipated over dinner. You had that same sweet smile, that unmistakable joyful laugh, that rouge on your cheeks when you blushed, and if that wasn't enough, that twinkle in your eyes when you looked at me.

MONDAY, NOVEMBER 25, 2024
THE NEW YORK TIMES

Regulator Sues Anti-Police Activist Who Spent Charity Funds on Himself
By David A. Fahrenthold
Arroyo Vista Inn

Text: Good morning, Sweetheart. *¡Ay, mi amor que tengas una hermosa mañana! Te marco más tarde. No pude dormir pensando en ti.* [Oh, my love, have a beautiful morning! I'll call you later. I couldn't sleep thinking of you.]

It was movie night, and you chose *A Walk in the Clouds*, a film that neither of us had watched in years. The question of who you'd watched this feature with popped in my mind, but it didn't matter; I'd watched it with someone too. It was a distant memory for me, so distant, I am not sure it had happened.

I looked forward to enjoying the movie with you, but not as much as I looked forward to being wrapped in your arms. We propped up the pillows, grabbed a blankie, and I melted into your arms like chocolate and marshmallows on a warm graham cracker.

The opening scene shows World War II soldier Paul Sutton arriving home from his tour with no one to greet him. He goes in search of his wife, only to discover she's hardly read any of the letters he wrote to her. This was a little personal to us both. I thought about the love letter I wrote to you but never gave you. The timing never seemed right. And I thought about the letter you gave me. A letter that, unlike Betty, I'd read many times over. Each time discovering something different I hadn't noticed before.

I sat there wondering if you'd ever write me another one and if you knew how much the one you wrote meant to me. My thoughts made me nervous, and instead, I made a joke of having placed the letter in a trunk like Betty had. We both laughed, but secretly I envied Betty and yearned for a trunk full of letters just like hers.

The letters weren't the only parallels between the screenplay and our story. The narrative's account of a woman who comes from a large, traditional, and well-established Mexican American family and falls in love with a man who can't say the same mirrors us in a way. In our case, however, you're the one who comes from the big family.

The film ended, and you pulled out a small envelope, placed it on the dresser, and asked me not to read it until morning. You'd written me another note. I was anxious to read it, but I waited patiently until morning like you asked.

Chapter 4

The Holidays
Las fiestas

Corazón,

Los días festivos de Gracias, de Navidad y del Año Nuevo son mis favoritos.

Siempre los pasamos con nuestros seres queridos. Escribiendo esta carta para ti, me puse triste y melancólico porque no puedo estar contigo para disfrutar tu compañía y tus deseos de estos días.

Me gustaría saber cómo los pasas y los has pasado. Todavía no hemos platicado de este tema a detalle.

Me recuerdo el primer día y la primera fiesta que me invitaste a tu casa. Me recuerdo del vino que me llevé, la gente que conocí, y de verte saliendo de cuarto en cuarto, de la cocina a la sala saludando y platicando con tus amigos, los invitados tal vez como yo y otras personas que iban llegando. Me hiciste sentir como parte de tu circulo íntimo de amigos y yo totalmente enamorado de ti y con más razón estando contigo en tu casa.

Me recuerdo de la segunda ves cuando lleve champurrado y pan dulce de nuestra tienda favorita, bueno eso todavía no se había declarado, lo digo porque allí fue donde disfrutamos nuestro primer champurrado y por poco el primer beso, casi porque todavía no era *tiempo. . .pero como quería, y los nervios, las ansias y temor de tu rechazo, porque en realidad me gustabas muchísimo, enamorado de ti, pero no quería que sufriera nuestra relación como amigos. Pero gracias te doy por los momentos iniciales que nunca olvidare de nuestro comienzo.*

Escribiendo esta carta y antes, me puse triste porque quiero disfrutar muchas más contigo especialmente estos días. Yo sé que me has dicho que los días festivos no los anhelas mucho, tal vez puedes decir más y como te sientes en estos días para saber más. Yo vengo de una familia extensa, crecimos poco a poco; tres, cinco, seis hasta nueve de familia con nuestros padres. Siempre con celebraciones en nuestra casa, con amigos y familiares. Puedes imaginarte el borlote que se armaba siempre estos días que sigue con mis hermanos hasta el día de hoy.

Lo triste que me pongo estos días, ahora que estamos de novios, y pienso en ti y que no estamos juntos, me dan ansias, pero me tranquilizo sabiendo que voy a tenerte en mis brazos pronto, tus besos, tus caricias comenzando con tus abrazos.

Te quiero mucho y más cada día,
Mis sentimientos no dejan de crecer,
Mis pensamientos no dejan de correr,
Mis deseos no dejan de cubrir lo mucho que te amo.
Te amo más que ayer,
Espero mañana porque te amo más que hoy . . .

[Sweetheart,

Thanksgiving, Christmas, and New Year's holidays are my favorites.

We always spend them with our loved ones. Writing this letter to you saddens me because I cannot be with you to enjoy your company and your wishes these days.

I would like to know how you spend them and have spent them. We have not yet discussed this topic in detail.

I remember the first time and the first party that you invited me to at your house. I remember the wine I brought, the people I met, and seeing you going from room to room, from the kitchen to the living room, greeting and chatting with your friends, guests maybe like me, and other people who arrived. You made me feel like part of your intimate circle of friends, and I was totally in love with you and even more so being with you in your house. I remember the second time when I brought champurrado and sweet bread from our favorite store. Well that had not yet been decided yet, I say this because that was where we enjoyed our first champurrado and almost had our first kiss, almost because it wasn't yet time. . . . I wanted to, but for the nerves, the anxiety, and the fear of your rejection, because, I liked you a lot; I was in love with you, but I didn't want our relationship as friends to suffer. But I thank you for the initial moments that I will never forget of our beginning.

Writing this letter, I became melancholic because I want to enjoy many more with you, especially these days. I know that you have told me that you don't look forward to the holidays very much, maybe you can tell me more and how you feel these days. I come from an extended family, and we grew little by little; three, five, six up to nine as a family with our parents. Always with celebrations in our house, with friends and family. You can imagine the fuss that always went on and continues with my brothers to this day.

How blue I get these days, now that we are dating, and I think about you and that we are not together, it makes me anxious, but I calm down knowing that I will have you in my arms soon, your kisses, your caresses, starting with your hugs.

I love you so much and more every day,
My feelings don't stop growing,
My thoughts don't stop running,
My wishes don't fail to show how much I love you.
I love you more than yesterday,
I wait for tomorrow because I love you more than today . . .]

TUESDAY, NOVEMBER 26, 2024
THE NEW YORK TIMES

Fugitive on List of FBI's Most-Wanted Terrorists Is Captured in UK
By Adeel Hassan
Stumptown Coffee Roasters, Pasadena

You invited me for tea, but the long workday called for something stronger, hot chocolate! The warm cocoa drink, prepared with whole milk, topped with sprinkled powder, and served in a sparkling white ceramic cup was almost enough to wash away the stress of the day.

The holidays had arrived, and it seemed like everyone needed a hot beverage, which meant the only available seats were outdoors. The evening was chilly, so I placed a legal pad on the metal patio chair as a buffer from the cold.

It wasn't any ordinary legal pad; it was my creative space. A place where my thoughts come to life, my life is documented, and my chronicles begin their journey. In your letter to me, you expressed sadness at the thought of not spending the holidays together. For me, it wasn't a thought, but a reality I've spent weeks preparing for. I knew I wouldn't be a guest at your dinner table, nor share a cocktail with you on Christmas Eve, nor open gifts with you on Christmas morning, but I wanted to make sure you had a special gift, one that couldn't be bought, but was created especially for you—your own book with your given name on the cover. You're a poet, a writer, and now an author, and the fact that you chose me to share your gift of writing speaks volumes.

WEDNESDAY, NOVEMBER 27, 2024
THE NEW YORK TIMES

Youth Pastor Charged with Nearly 200 Sex Crimes Going Back Decades
By Billy Witz

Altadena Crest Trail Cobb Estate Trailhead, Altadena

Late this afternoon, we began our third attempt to reach the waterfall. Within minutes, I noticed that you were in much better shape than you were just a few weeks ago. Your breathing was steady, your stride more confident, and you certainly didn't stop to kiss me as often.

You brought up how nervous you were the day you asked me to be your girlfriend and joked about how I probably didn't remember. I smiled and looked away. Not only did I remember, but I also had every beautiful detail written down and documented.

It had been almost two and a half weeks, but it felt like we had never left. We arrived at the spot where you asked me and bumped into a group of returning hikers. You asked them how much further it was to reach the chute, to which they responded .2 miles. I couldn't believe how close we'd come. Shortly thereafter, we arrived at an opening with a clear shallow pool, a fairy tale cascade, and a boulder that tittered precariously up above. It was probably the world's longest proposal, which finally culminated with a soft kiss and a long-awaited embrace in front of the falls.

WEDNESDAY, NOVEMBER 27, 2024 (CONTINUED)

There's a bench composed of Arroyo Seco rocks that sits above the Rose Bowl, overlooking the golf course. One of the stones has been engraved with the word "imagine." I sat there and meditated many times before I knew you'd come into my life. I shared it with you one night several months ago. We walked up the hill under the light of the moon, and you pointed to the celestial orb just above our heads and remarked how majestic it was. You brought me back to it this evening, and you referred to it as our bench. Imagine that!

FRIDAY, NOVEMBER 29, 2024
THE NEW YORK TIMES

Syrian Rebels Breach City of Aleppo, in Biggest Advance in Years
By Raja Abdulrahim

Text: *¡Cada momento que estoy alegado de ti es cómo un castigo que no entiendo! ¿Me pregunto qué estará haciendo mi amor? ¿Que está pensando cuando no estamos juntos? Mis pensamientos se van a las nubes y me tengo que detener porque si no me vuelvo loco hasta la próxima vez que esté contigo mi amor. ¡La distancia mentalmente me llena de ansias, pero tus mensajes me calman un montón porque sé que ya pronto te voy a tener en mis brazos!*

> *Te adoro*

[Text: Every moment that I am away from you is like a punishment that I don't understand! I wonder what my love is doing. What is she thinking when we are not together? My thoughts go to the clouds, and I must stop because if not, I will go crazy until the next time I am with you, my love. The distance fills me with anxiety, but your messages calm me because I know that soon I will have you in my arms!

> I adore you.]

Response:

Mi vida,

> *Todo lo que hago lo hago porque tu vives en mis pensamientos. El desayuno que disfruté esta mañana, me lo comí sabiendo que tú también disfrutabas el tuyo. El ejercicio que hice, lo hice para acompañarte. El piano que practique fue para poder tocar algo lindo para ti. Las hojas que escribí fueron porque tú eres mi inspiración. Y los pasos que baile fueron porque algún día me gustaría compartirlos contigo. Así que con esto espero que no tengas ninguna duda que yo también la paso pensando en ti. Te quiero*

[My love,

Everything I do I do because you live in my thoughts. The breakfast I enjoyed this morning, I ate knowing that you enjoyed yours too. The exercise I did, I did to accompany you. The piano I practiced was so I could play something nice for you. The paragraphs I wrote were because you are my inspiration. And the steps I danced were because one day I would like to share them with you. So, with this, I hope you have no doubt that I also spend time thinking of you. I love you]

SATURDAY, NOVEMBER 30, 2024
PASADENA STAR-NEWS

In shock offensive, insurgents breach largest Syrian City
By Sarah El Deeb

Text: *¡Mi corazón cada vez que nos encontramos me enseñas algo nuevo de ti y me retiro de tu lado más enamorado de ti!*
[Sweetheart, every time we meet, you teach me something new about yourself, and I leave your side more in love with you!]

Response: *Espero que siga descubriendo novedades mías al igual que yo siga descubriendo las suyas.*
[I hope you continue discovering things about me just as I continue discovering things about you.]

Text: *¡Lo bonito de nuestra relación es que nunca quiero parar de descubrir novedades mutuas para seguir creciendo infinitamente contigo!*
[The beautiful thing about our relationship is that I never want to stop discovering things about one another to continue growing infinitely with you!]

SUNDAY, DECEMBER 1, 2024
PASADENA STAR-NEWS

Russia advances in Eastern Ukraine, captures villages
By Constant Méheut

Text: *No dejo de pensar en ti—Espero con ansias de hablar contigo más tarde. Te quiero mucho.* [I can't stop thinking about you—I look forward to talking with you later. I love you very much.]

MONDAY, DECEMBER 2, 2024
THE NEW YORK TIMES

American Thought to Be Alive in Gaza Was Killed on Oct. 7, Israel Says
By Liam Stack
Açai Bar, Pasadena

Text: Baby what would you like from Açaí Bowl?
Response: Only if you get one for you.
Text: Yes! What would you like?
Response: One protein shake with everything thank you.
Text: Anything for my girl.

It's always nice to receive a text message from you, but it's even nicer when it comes with the prospect of seeing you. My colleague and I were out on the field shopping for the department holiday party. The event we'd been planning for months had arrived, and we'd tasked ourselves with the final details. We roamed the aisles of one of the city's big chain stores and scoured the shelves of floor-to-ceiling merchandise for holiday décor, gift wrap, and stocking stuffers.

It looked like Christmas, but it didn't smell, sound, or feel like Christmas. The seasonal store I grew up with was Stats. More than a retailer, it was a destination. It was an outing where my parents took relatives who visited from Guatemala, the one shop where my mom could find proper *musgo* for her nativity scene, and more importantly, it was a place where my imagination soared.

Housed in an unassuming one-story brick building behind two sets of glass doors was a world where day turned into night, snow fell continuously but never covered the ground, Christmas songs played uninterrupted, and the aromas of gingerbread and peppermint permeated throughout. The structure itself was a remnant of the famous Castle Green built in 1898 and was barely saved from complete demolition in 1935.

As a child, I looked forward to walking through its doors and feeling the warmth as if the fireplace had been burning all day. The decorative garlands, poinsettias, and twinkly lights blended seamlessly with the Victorian-era ceiling beams, round and square columns with ornamented capitals, and flattened horseshoe-arched doorways. It wasn't a store; it was the North Pole. It was a place where imagination, fantasy, and magic thrived for Santa's helpers, who worked tirelessly to answer letters addressed to Jolly Old Saint Nick himself.

With as much pen palling as I did when I was a kid, I don't remember ever having penned a letter to Santa. I attempted to stay up many times and catch the big guy placing the gifts under the tree, but I fell asleep every time. I was certain his elves blew sleep dust all over the world's children. By the time the effects of the snooze concoction wore off, the presents had already been placed neatly under the tree.

I'd run over and gawk at the beautifully wrapped gifts and kick myself because I knew I had to wait another year for a chance to see *Papa Noël*.

Hmmm! Well, you're never too old to write a letter to Santa.

Dear Santa,

How are things in the North Pole? Have the elves been naughty or nice? Is Rudolph's nose still red?

I am writing to you because I have been a very good girl this year. I finished my one-year confirmation program, I took really good care of my dad, and I planted a garden at work for my peers to enjoy. In return, I am asking for one little thing, an extra special boyfriend.

I would like a beau who smiles when he sees me, laughs at my jokes, and brings me hot chocolate on a cold day. And if it's not too much to ask, I would like a fella who writes me little love notes, watches movies with me, and wants to dance with me as much as I want to dance with him.

I know you are busy putting the final touches on all your gifts, but I want to thank you for taking my request into consideration. I look forward to your visit, and as always, I will leave a plate of homemade chocolate chip cookies and a glass of cold milk by the tree.

Merry Christmas!

Well, how about that, Kris Kringle knew exactly what I wanted for Christmas, and he dropped him off early this year. Maybe if I can stay awake, I can thank him in person next Christmas.

Text: *Corazón, como siempre, me dejaste sin aliento cuando te vi. ¡Y loco por abrasarte y besarte!*

[Sweetheart, as always, you left me breathless when I saw you. And with a crazy urge to hug you and kiss you!]

Image: I was late to be your first love, but just in time to be your last.

Response: *Hola mi amor. Me encanto verte esta tarde, aunque solo fueron unos instantes. Anhelo el momento que nos volvamos a ver.*

[Hello my love. I loved seeing you this afternoon, although it was only for a few moments. I long for the moment when we meet again.]

Text: *A mí también. Te mirabas tan hermosa mi amor. Use casi toda mi fuerza para evitar una escena de besos y un abrazo en ese lugar. Yo anhelo verte pronto.*

[Me too. You looked so beautiful, my love. I used all my strength to avoid a kissing and hugging scene at that place. I long to see you soon.]

Response: *Me hubiera encantado que me tomara en sus brazos.*
[I would have loved for you to have taken me in your arms.]

Text: *¡A mí también corazoncito!*
[Me too, sweetheart!]

Chapter 5

Distance Makes the Heart Grow Fonder

La ausencia es el amor lo que el fuego es el aire: apaga el pequeño y aviva el grande

WEDNESDAY, DECEMBER 4, 2024
THE NEW YORK TIMES

Gunman Shoots 2 Kindergarteners at Rural Christian School in Targeted Attack
By Hank Sanders; Alexandra E. Petri

I only saw you briefly this afternoon, but it was just enough time to hand me a short letter that read, *No leas hasta mañana.*

Text: *Como te amo mi corazón.*
[How I love you sweetheart.]

Response: *Yo te amo a ti mi vida.*
[I love you, my love.]

Text: *¡Te extrañare mucho! ¡Pero usare este tiempo para apreciarte más!* [I will miss you very much! But I will use this time to appreciate you more!]

Response: *No te preocupes mi vida, el tiempo pasa rápido.* [Don't worry sweetheart, time passes quickly.]

Text: *¡Eso sí! Como dice la canción: El tiempo pasa, y no te puedo olvidar.*[1] *Te traigo en mis pensamientos constantemente mi amor.* [Yes! As the song says: Time passes, and I can't forget you.[2] You're in my thoughts constantly, my love.]

Response: *Me da mucha ternura saber qué piensas en mí. Verás que pronto me tendrás de nuevo en tus brazos.*
[It comforts me that you think of me. You'll see that you'll have me back in your arms soon . . .]

THURSDAY, DECEMBER 5, 2024
THE PASADENA STAR-NEWS

CEO Shot to Death, Gunman at Large
By Jake Offenhartz; Kren Matthews; Michael R. Slsak
THE ASSOCIATED PRESS

4 de diciembre 2024

Mi amor,

Siempre pensando en ti y la próxima ves que te voy a besar y abrasar. Mis pensamientos corren locos cuando sé que voy a estar lejos de ti.

---

1. Lyrics from the song "Triste Recuerdo" by Antonio Aguilar. Wikipedia, "Antonio Aguilar."
2. Lyrics from the song "Triste Recuerdo" by Antonio Aguilar. Wikipedia, "Antonio Aguilar."

Tú me haces sentir feliz física y emocionalmente con todos los abrazos y besos que me das. Estas breves palabras no pueden comenzar a decirte lo mucho que te quiero y te voy a extrañar estos días. Me da mucho gusto que te vez alegre por los eventos que vas a asistir, y quiero mucho que disfrutes.

Te quiero y te amo

[December 4, 2024

My love,

I am always thinking of you, and the next time, I'm going to kiss and hug you. My thoughts run crazy when I know I'm going to be away from you.

You make me feel happy physically and emotionally with all the hugs and kisses you give me. These few words cannot begin to tell you how much I love you, and I am going to miss you these days. I am very pleased that you are happy about the events you are going to attend, and I really want you to enjoy them.

I love you]

FRIDAY, DECEMBER 6, 2024
THE NEW YORK TIMES

Man Who Kidnapped Woman From Bloomberg's Colorado Ranch Gets 22 Years in Prison
By Hank Sanders

Text: I want to tell you that I'm so in love with you! I'm glad it [the party] went well. The excitement in your voice is what I wanted to hear. Your team worked hard to bring it together. *Besitos.*

SATURDAY, DECEMBER 7, 2024
LOS ANGELES TIMES

Son of killer is arrested in teen's slaying; Zuberi Sharp, 24, is accused of a hacking death similar to his father's crime in 2007.
By Noah Goldberg; Richard Winton

Text: *¡El amor debe ser como el café—fuerte, caliente y a diario! ¿Qué piensas mi corazón? ¿Estas Escribiendo?* [Love should be like coffee—strong, hot, and daily! What are you thinking my love? Are you writing?]

Response: I just finished one handwritten page that I'm happy with and now I'm getting ready to run the Rose Bowl. *Pero si pensando en ti.* [But yes, thinking about you.]

Text. Awesome! I need to work on my running! It took me 40 minutes to run three miles. Tell me how it goes for you Baby.

Response: That's beautiful. Maybe we can add a 2025 5K to our Bucket List?

Text: Yes! I can't wait to pick one with you.

It's been a few weeks since we added an item to our bucket list, and a 5K seems like the perfect new addition for us both. I'm training for a run in April, and this also fits well with your fitness goals.

I was never a runner, and I never understood how something that in many ways was painful to me, appealed to so many others. In July of 2022, I lost a very good friend of mine, and grieving the loss of someone who had been such a big part of my life began to take a toll on me physically and mentally. A few days after his passing, I went for a walk, but I quickly became overwhelmed with emotions, and the tears began to roll down my face. I didn't want anyone to see me, so I started running. The overexertion caused me to hyperventilate, but I noticed the wind dried my tears, and little by little, I began to calm down. I finally understood why so many people practice a sport that I spent so many years running away from.

Text: *Mi amor, cuando estoy tan lejos de ti y sé que no puedo ir a verte por la distancia, me pongo a pensar en lo mucho que te extraño y que te quiero. Las cosas tan sencillas como escuchar tu voz en persona o tenerte cerca y sabiendo que puedo extender mis manos y tomar las tuyas para abrazarte sin dejarte por un largo tiempo para sentir tu calor y tu aroma tan dulce y sensual. ¡Me trae una sonrisa sabiendo que ya proto estaremos juntos enlazados con un beso muy tierno y profundo!*

[My love, when I am so far from you and I know that I cannot go see you because of the distance, I start to think about how much I miss you and that I love you. Something as precious as hearing your voice in person or having you close and knowing that I can reach out and take your hands to hug you to feel your warmth and sweet sensual aroma. It brings a smile to my face knowing that we will soon be together joined by a very tender kiss!]

Response: *Cariño, mi corazón te anhela. Voy a pasar estos días un poco ocupada para que me duela un poco menos el corazón por ti. Hago ejercicio, escribo y toco el piano, pero todavía es difícil no pensar en ti cuando hago esas cosas. Dicen que la distancia hace crecer el cariño y quizás sea cierto. Te extraño mucho y me consuela saber que sientes lo mismo. Hasta que nos volvamos a ver, estaré pensando en todas las cosas que haces que me hacen sonreír.*

[Sweetheart, my heart longs for you. I'm going to spend these days a little busy so that my heart hurts a little less for you. I exercise, write, and play the piano, but it's still hard not to think of you when I do those things. They say that distance makes the heart grow fonder and perhaps it is true. I miss you so much, and it comforts me to know that you feel the same. Until we meet again, I'll be thinking of all the things you do that make me smile.]

SUNDAY, DECEMBER 8, 2024
PASADENA STAR-NEWS

Pearl Harbor Memories Still Fresh for Vet
By Anissa Rivera

Text: *Mañana regreso mi amor—no puedo esperar para verte y abrazarte.* [I'll be back tomorrow my love—I can't wait to see you and hold you.]

MONDAY, DECEMBER 9, 2024
PASADENA STAR-NEWS

Thousands in Bangladesh Protest Attacks in India
THE ASSOCIATED PRESS

Text: 3.1 miles 37.5 minutes. Right behind you Baby. *Muy buenos días mi corazón.* [Good morning my love.]

Your text message was soon followed by a short call. We have an agreement that you call when missing me becomes too much for you to bear. I've been busy since we last saw each other, writing, working, and wondering if you're thinking about me.

I thought about you this morning when I put on my red coat. I don't wear it often, but I clearly remember the first time you saw me wearing it and my matching red lipstick. We weren't dating yet when you called with the pretense that you were in the area and wanted to stop by and say hello.

You may have been eager to see me, but when you saw me, your self-assurance quickly dwindled. I felt your energy, like I did that night in the Vallarta Supermarket parking lot. You gave me a hug, we spoke briefly, you looked at me with those big bashful eyes, you turned away, and just like that, you left.

I know how you felt that afternoon after that second failed first-kiss attempt because at that very moment, your soul tugged at mine.

Chapter 6

Lover's Spats
Riñas de amantes

Celestino Ristorante & Bar, Pasadena

Text: Boo
Response: Ahhh!

Seeing you after a long separation felt like I had to get to know you all over again. At dinner tonight, I was reintroduced to you, your sweet smile, and your warm embrace. You took note of my nervous energy and allowed me to go on about the mishaps I experienced during the days you were gone, like almost losing my stilettos and cowboy hat. That's a story for another day.

For our long-awaited reunion, you chose a well-liked local *ristorante*, and we opted for the outdoor seating under the comforting warmth of the ceiling-mounted heaters. The vinyl patio enclosure reminded me of the restaurants in Paris and Rome during the rainy season. The otherwise alfresco dining areas are completely covered in see-through plastic so diners can continue enjoying their savory dishes despite inclement weather. All we needed was the sight of sliding raindrops as they peeked in to see what we were doing. And if raindrops could talk, they'd whisper about a scene that is quite common in those parts, two lovestruck lovers reveling in each other's presence as if they were meeting for the first time.

Our maître d' wore an impeccable white button shirt, black bow tie, and neatly pressed black slacks. His intermittent visits to our table were sprinkled with accented *grazies* and *pregos* that made me feel like we were somewhere other than Lake Avenue.

You waited patiently as I rattled off the last of my nonsense topics for your turn to speak. You wanted to discuss something more serious, like the voice message I left you while you were away. You wanted to better understand the points I made, why I made them, and even my tone of voice. I was uncomfortable discussing those things with you. I somehow just expected you to understand.

You weren't just asking for clarification; I'd hurt you, and you wanted to know why. I didn't quite have a response for you other than the response I couldn't verbalize, which was that I was protecting myself. You often bring up the topic of connection, and I do whatever I can for you to feel connected to me; however, I don't always feel connected to you, and it's easier for me to disconnect mentally and emotionally during an absence.

Moreover, I'd ask you not to share the details of your trip, but you insisted, and you told me anyway. Your reasoning was that I should know in case something should happen to you on one of your trips. This trip was in the past, so I was at a loss as to why you told me.

I, too, had thoughts about the same scenario when applied to me. What if something happened to me and you never had a chance to read my thoughts? The idea crossed my mind to simply give you my diary or ask someone to give it to you should something happen; however, I usually vacate those thoughts from my mind as quickly as they move in.

We continued becoming reacquainted during our *cena* of spinach salad, tomato pasta, and medium grilled steak. We enjoyed our *pasto* to the slow and steady rhythm of our *rendezvous*, and although some issues were left unresolved, you made sure we took some steps in the right direction.

WEDNESDAY, DECEMBER 11, 2024
THE NEW YORK TIMES

Health Insurance Workers Fearful Amid Public Anger after Slaying of CEO
By Reed Abelson; Mitch Smith; Katie Benner; Amy Julia Harris

Text: Good morning, Baby! *¡Gracias por la sonrisa de esta mañana que me distes! ¡Pensando en ti!* [Thank you for the smile you gave me this morning! Thinking of you!]

The *sonrisa* you referred to was the smile you told me you have every morning when you wake up thinking of me. I woke up thinking of you as well. I wondered what time you'd text me to wish me a good morning and if I'd be seeing you today. Part of me knew I wouldn't be seeing you. I was full of dread and knew something was wrong. Even your text messages were off, but I didn't want to dwell on something that only existed in my imagination, so I did my best to ignore it.

THURSDAY, DECEMBER 12, 2024
THE NEW YORK TIMES

DEI Official at University of Michigan Is Fired Over Antisemitism Claim, Lawyer Says
By Stephanie Saul; Vimal Patel

When I saw your missed call this morning, I knew there was an issue. I returned your call only to hear you tell me one of your family members wasn't well, and you were no longer available to be my plus-one this evening. For a moment, I thought it was a cruel joke, until I realized you were serious.

I came out of a twenty-five-year relationship with someone who was rarely my plus-one, and when he was, he made me wish he wasn't. To say that I am sensitive to cancellations is an understatement, and this would be your third cancellation in our short time together.

You were extremely apologetic, but regardless of the circumstances, I couldn't stop myself from feeling hurt. My stomach tightened up, my mouth became dry, and I took a deep breath to hold back my tears. More heartbreaking than the pain I felt was the loss of trust. It took me a long time to get the courage to ask you to be my plus-one, and now, a gala, a Christmas party, and a comedy show later, I've exhausted my asks.

I texted you to please respect my wishes and not attend my piano recital on Sunday. It's not that I don't want you there, but I don't want to put myself through three days of anxiety wondering if you'll attend.

FRIDAY, DECEMBER 13, 2024
PASADENA STAR-NEWS

Fight ended in fatal shooting of Covina man
By Ruby Gonzales

Mi preciosa y querida novia,

Estos días han sido muy pesados, pero también han abierto, yo pienso heridas que tal vez ambos cargamos.

Ayer jueves lamente muchísimo como te decía que no podía ir contigo al evento, porque sabía que te iba disgustar mucho, bueno eso paso. No pude decir, ni hacerte saber lo mucho que me dolió y yo sé por tu mensaje que te hice mucho daño emocionalmente.

Yo no quiero, nunca, si es posible hacerte ninguna clase de daño, se emocional, física o mental. Yo sé que emos hablado, pero no hemos discutido a detalle como ser mejores para ambos en todos niveles.

Estos días pensando en ti y nuestro tiempo juntos, de todo lo que hemos hecho y todo lo que queremos hacer juntos o individualmente. Cuando pasan cosas como lo que paso este jueves, yo pienso que pone nuestra relación al punto y nos dice, a mi pues, que tengo que poner más atención en las necesidades de nuestra relación y el futuro de nuestras ambiciones juntos.

*Nuestra relación y estar contigo es muy importante para mí.
Yo no pienso y no quiero causarte ninguna clase de dolor, si no, yo
quiero llenarte de felicidad y amor. Siempre . . .*

*Lo que si se, es que te quiero mucho y te amo con toda mi
alma. Mis pensamientos están en ti constantemente. Te llevo en mi
corazón, todo lo que hago, lo hago pensando de ti y como te gustaría
esto o esta cosa o este lugar. Ya dicho, el amor duele, duele cuando te
hago daño y te causo coraje y angustia. No quiero para ti eso.*

*Mira, yo sé que nuestra relación no es lo que nosotros queremos
totalmente, pero quiero hacer lo más posible para tenerte a mi lado.
Tu eres mi pasión y me llevas a niveles que yo anhelo con el amor y
las caricias que me das espero que yo te doy lo mismo y quiero seguir
haciéndolo mi vida.*

*Quiero evitar cualquier daño y quiero darte la felicidad que
mereces. Yo sé que se toma mucho esfuerzo, pero estoy dispuesto
hacer la lucha para poner y dejar esa sonrisa de la cual mucho me
enamore el día que nos encontramos en aquel café, me enamore de
ti y espero que tu sigas enamorada de mí, porque para mí, mi amor
crece cada día para ti.*

Con mucho amor y mucho cariño.

[My beautiful and dear girlfriend,

These days have been very heavy, but they have also opened,
I think, wounds that perhaps we both carry.

Yesterday, Thursday, I was very sorry as I told you that I
couldn't go with you to the event, and I knew that you would be
very upset, well that happened. I couldn't say or let you know how
much it hurt me, and I know from your message that I hurt you a
lot emotionally.

I do not want, ever, if possible, to cause you any kind of pain, be
it emotional, physical, or mental. I know we've talked, but we haven't
discussed in detail how to be better for both of us on all levels.

These days, I think about you and our time together, about
everything we have done and everything we want to do together or
individually. When things happen like what happened this Thursday, I think it brings our relationship to a point and tells us, well,

that I must pay more attention to the needs of our relationship and the future of our ambitions together.

Our relationship and being with you is very important to me. I don't think, and I don't want to cause any kind of pain. I want to fill you with happiness and love. Always . . .

What I do know is that I love you very much, and I love you with all my soul. My thoughts are on you constantly. I carry you in my heart; everything I do, I do it thinking about you and how you would like this or that thing or place. Already said, love hurts, it hurts when I hurt you and cause you anger and anguish. I don't want that for you.

Look, I know that our relationship is not what we totally want, but I want to do everything possible to have you by my side. You are my passion, and you take me to levels that I long for with the love and caresses you give me. I hope that I give you the same and I want to continue doing that in my life.

I want to avoid harming you, and I want to give you the happiness you deserve. I know that it takes a lot of effort, but I am willing to fight to put on and leave that smile that I fell in love with the day we met in that café, I fell in love with you, and I hope that you continue to fall in love with me, because for me, my love grows every day for you.

With a lot of love and affection.]

SATURDAY, DECEMBER 14, 2024
THE NEW YORK TIMES

Syria Shudders as Assad's Prison Atrocities Come Into the Light
By Christina Goldbaum
Hollywood Piano, Pasadena

I uninvited you to my piano recital, but you were determined to show up and support me. I wasn't nervous about seeing you nor performing until I found out on arrival that I'd be playing on a

$400,000 nine-foot Steingraeber & Söhne[3] concert piano. After eight years of learning to play, I still consider myself a beginner, and the thought of even touching a piano that was worth twice as much as the base price of a Mercedes-Maybach S-Class made me nauseous. When I learned you'd be there, I spent the day practicing "Sabrina" by N. Jane Tan and "Greensleeves." I didn't want to disappoint you.

We walked in together, and you'd already met the store manager, who escorted us over to the recital area. And there it was, in all its glory, shellacked in the glossiest of black coats that made my patent leather heels appear dull. I stopped within a few feet of it as if I were asking it permission to approach. I didn't; I did, however, ask the store manager, who allowed me to take it for a test drive. I sat in front of the ivories and ran my fingers over them. Even the texture was different; it felt like freshly cut marble. After holding my breath for a few moments, I began to press down on the keys that moved like a knife cutting into artisanal butter from Brittany. My first thought: no one's going to hear my mistakes on this!

I was the third to perform, and although I fumbled, I was happy I didn't crash and burn. And there you were, sitting in the front row, taking pictures of me, with a huge smile on your face. You looked as if I had just finished playing "Moonlight Sonata" by Ludwig van Beethoven. When I finished, we sat together and enjoyed the remaining performances, mostly children. The organizer closed the program with a "Rudolph the Red-Nosed Reindeer" sing-along. I guess Rudolph's nose is still red! As we got up to leave, you turned to the dessert table, not to grab a cookie, but to reach for a bouquet of a dozen red roses you'd left earlier that day.

The crimson blooms came beautifully wrapped in paper printed with the word "love." The thoughtful gift made me feel like a celebrity, but more importantly, I felt like your leading lady. You came prepared with another gift, the book *I Love You, Ronnie: The Letters of Ronald Reagan to Nancy Reagan*, and more special to me, a handwritten letter. We spoke briefly at the close of the evening,

3. Major German manufacturer of grand and upright pianos. The family business was founded 1852 in Bayreuth. Wikipedia, "Steingraeber & Söhne."

and you told me you wanted to fill up my drawer with letters, and I can't tell you how much I loved the idea. The letter was dated Friday, December 13, the day after our spat. In it, you wrote that you hoped that I continued to fall in love with you, to which I responded that I was very much in love with you and that I loved you with all my heart.

MONDAY, DECEMBER 16, 2024
LOS ANGELES TIMES

TED WEIANT, 1947–2024; Famed for 16-month run of "Love Letters"; The LA theater director also helped develop the work of new playwrights.
By Ashley Lee

I never begin writing with the intention of writing a book. You asked me if I knew how the story ended, and quite honestly, I wasn't sure about its beginning or middle. I did know, however, how many pages I wanted to write. I began with a time frame of October 1 to December 31, 2024, which was roughly ninety days. I tend to be more disciplined when I give myself a time span. I saw those initial pages as the first half or at least the first third of whatever this creative outlet would become. I never imagined these ninety pages would encompass a beginning, middle, and end.

Coincidentally, ninety pages are the average number for a novella, a book that is longer than a short story and shorter than a novel. Its name is reminiscent of the *novelas* I grew up watching. Unlike their English counterparts that were televised for a lifetime, *novelas* were usually on-air for a few short months and sometimes for more than one year.

They all explore the most common story themes of love, good versus evil, coming of age, redemption, courage, revenge, and family, with an emphasis on the Cinderella archetype. The narrative typically tells a story of a poor girl who meets a rich guy, or vice versa, they fall in love, the antagonist tries to break them up, but somehow their plan is foiled and the couple lives happily ever after.

Among my favorite nighttime soaps were the 1986 to 1987 Venezuelan telenovela *Cristal* and the 1993 Mexican telenovela *Corazón Salvaje*. I was just ten years old when *Cristal* aired, and the scene where the two main characters see each other for the first time was so poignant; I still remember it to this day.

Cristal, an aspiring model, works for Luis's mom, an icon of the fashion world. One day, Luis enters a fashion show in progress, and just as Cristal pivots on the runway, they lock eyes for the first time. It's unclear to me whether *el amor a primera vista* is a pause in real time or if the interlude is the result of a philter; what is clear is that it's a perfect example of love at first sight.

I was sick with vertigo the first time you and I met, so it was difficult for me to focus. I do remember, however, our first special date on a warm July afternoon. I wore a 1950s-inspired black halter, high-low dress, with large white polka dots that you gifted me. I let my hair down, put on some mascara and bright red French lipstick. You stepped out of your car and walked over to me. You were nicely dressed in a buttoned-up shirt and slacks, and we held our gaze on one another as if we were falling in love for the first time. Your hands trembled as you reached for me; you gave me a delicate embrace, a nervous smile, and an equally soft kiss to keep my lipstick from smudging. It's by far one of my favorite moments with you.

As predictable as the soap story arches were and still are, their popularity hasn't waned. Daughters, moms, *abuelitas*, and now even dads and brothers spend hours on Univision watching tales of love, courtship, and romance. They remind us of that special someone we once had, they incite us to daydream of the endless possibilities, and give hope to those looking, that someday they too will find the one.

In the final scene of *Corazón Salvaje*, Juan is on the bluff with Monica, who is wearing an off-the-shoulder lace ball gown reminiscent of Cinderella herself. We never find out what happens after the final kissing scene of this or any soap opera, but it's presumed that they live happily ever after.

El Fin [The End]

Bibliography

"Antonio Aguilar." Wikipedia, April 8, 2025. https://en.wikipedia.org/wiki/Antonio_Aguilar.

Duchesse, Anastascia. *Dabresha Goes to France: An Urban Girl's Adventure Outside of Her Comfort Zone*. US: Chateau Foveo, 2016.

"Gilligan's Island." Wikipedia, May 5, 2025. https://en.wikipedia.org/wiki/Gilligan%27s_Island.

"June Marlowe." Wikipedia, February 28, 2025. https://en.wikipedia.org/wiki/June_Marlowe.

"Lady and the Tramp." Wikipedia, April 18, 2025. https://en.wikipedia.org/wiki/Lady_and_the_Tramp.

"Little Johnny." Wikipedia, March 2, 2025. https://en.wikipedia.org/wiki/Little_Johnny.

"Los Angeles County Metropolitan Transportation Authority." Wikipedia, April 5, 2025. https://en.wikipedia.org/wiki/Los_Angeles_County_Metropolitan_Transportation_Authority.

"Steingraeber & Söhne." Wikipedia, October. 5, 2023. https://en.wikipedia.org/wiki/Steingraeber_%26_S%C3%B6hne.

"Vallarta Supermarkets." Wikipedia, December 21, 2024. https://en.wikipedia.org/wiki/Vallarta_Supermarkets.